THE MISUNDERSTANDINGS OF NIA

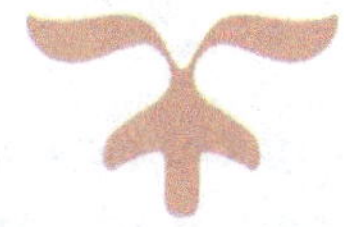

BY:

LAADIE OHH

Laadie Ohh Publishing

Dedication

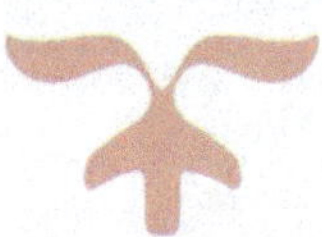

For my three roses,
whose light, laughter, and love remind me that
beauty still grows after every storm.
You are the reason I keep writing, keep
believing, keep blooming.
Every page carries a petal of your inspiration.

The Sound of Rain

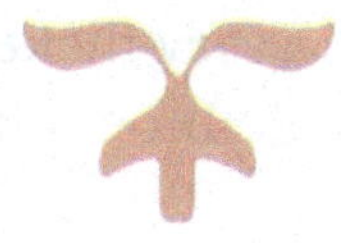

The rain came down in sheets the morning they laid Laneshia Stanson to rest.

Atlanta skies had a way of weeping when hearts did, and that morning, the clouds hung low over Auburn Avenue, swollen and gray, like heaven itself had come close enough to feel the ache. The city moved slower than usual. Traffic lights blurred through the drizzle; umbrellas bloomed like dark flowers. Inside the sanctuary of The Rebuild Project, the scent of lilies and damp earth mingled with candle wax and the lingering sweetness of Laneshia's perfume. The one she'd worn on Sundays. That soft, familiar trace of jasmine and cedar.

Nia Daniels stood near the altar; hands clasped so tightly the skin around her knuckles blanched. She wasn't crying...not yet. She had already cried enough for two lifetimes. The long night at the hospital, the hours of calls that followed, the quiet drive home where grief came in gasps so sharp they burned. Now, all that remained was a kind of hollow stillness. A silence that didn't soothe.

The Rebuild sanctuary, once alive with laughter, tambourines, and Laneshia's booming encouragement, felt unbearably still. The storm outside made the windows hum, as if the building itself was mourning. Every flicker of lightning painted the walls a pale blue, like memory trying to take shape.

"She would've hated all this fuss," Nia thought, her gaze fixed on the framed portrait at the front of the pulpit. Laneshia's smile beamed in that photo, full of light and defiance. That same smile had coaxed Nia off the back pew years ago, when she was still hiding behind shame and self-doubt.
Now, that smile stared back from glossy paper...forever stilled...forever unreachable.

Bishop Calloway's voice echoed from the podium, deep and practiced. He was speaking about legacy, about purpose, about running the race well. Nia heard the words but couldn't hold on to them. They drifted through the fog of her grief like leaves in rainwater. Visible, but impossible to grasp.

"And we know that her vision will continue through those she mentored, those she poured herself into," the bishop said, his eyes sweeping over the room. They landed on Nia for a fraction too long.
Her breath hitched.
She wasn't ready for that look. Not yet.

Everyone in the room already knew it. Laneshia had named Nia Daniels as her successor in The Rebuild Project's final charter. A quiet transition signed and witnessed only weeks before the illness took her. It was supposed to be a joyful passing of the torch. Instead, it felt like an inheritance she hadn't earned. A crown that weighed more than she could carry.

Thunder rolled over the roof like a slow drumbeat. Nia looked up. Through the stained-glass window behind the pulpit, lightning flashed across the figure of a dove mid-flight.
Peace in motion.
Freedom caught in stillness.
It reminded her of Laneshia's last words, whispered from a hospital bed surrounded by machines that hummed like prayers.

"Don't be afraid of becoming what God already saw in you, baby. Even storms make things grow."

Nia blinked, and the memory dissolved into the present again. People were standing now, filing past the casket with flowers and trembling hands. Some whispered "Rest well, Pastor," others just wept. When it was Nia's turn, she froze halfway down the aisle. The polished mahogany seemed to ripple in the candlelight, and in it, she saw her own reflection. Eyes swollen, mouth set, and heart split open.
The mirror motif she would come to know too well.

For the first time, the reality struck. Laneshia was gone, and every reflection of her from now on would live through Nia's actions.

Not her words. Not her lessons.
Her actions.

She laid a single rose, a pale pink one, on the coffin. The same kind Laneshia used to keep in a vase on her office desk. It was crushed slightly from her grip, but beautiful still. The petals glistened with raindrops from her coat sleeve, and Nia whispered beneath her breath:

"I'll try."

It wasn't a promise, not yet. Just a fragile attempt at courage.
And as thunder cracked once more above the sanctuary, something within her shifted—small, unsteady, but real. The beginning of obedience, maybe. Or the beginning of surrender.

The sanctuary emptied slowly, like a tide pulling away from shore. Hushed voices, careful embraces, the rustle of umbrellas shaking off rain. Each sound felt too sharp, too ordinary, against the weight of what had just happened.

Nia lingered near the front pew until the last of the mourners drifted out. She couldn't bring herself to move, not yet. The church lights had been dimmed to a soft gold, shadows stretching long across the aisles. Outside, the storm had quieted to a mist, but the thunder still rolled far in the distance. Low, steady, like a pulse.

Her pulse.

On the pulpit, the large white binder marked THE REBUILD PROJECT VISION 2001–2020 sat beneath a silk cloth. It had been Laneshia's heartbeat in paper form. Pages filled with sermons, budgets, outreach plans, dreams scribbled in margins. Nia's name appeared in neat cursive handwriting across several tabs, each marking the programs she'd once helped coordinate. Seeing her name there now felt foreign, as though it belonged to someone stronger, someone braver.

A knock at the sanctuary door startled her. "Hey," came a voice, soft and careful.

It was Tasha, her closest friend and one of the few people who could enter Nia's silence without breaking it. She still wore her usher's uniform, her hair damp from the rain, mascara slightly smudged under kind eyes.

"They're waiting for you downstairs," Tasha said, stepping closer. "The board wants to go over the transition plans. Just a few signatures."

Nia exhaled. "Already?"

Tasha hesitated. "They said it was what Pastor Laneshia wanted. She had it all set up."

Nia looked up at the ceiling, as if heaven might intervene. "She planned everything. Even this moment."

"She trusted you for a reason."

"I wish I knew what that reason was."

Tasha's hand found hers, warm and steady. "You do. You've just been too humble to believe it."

That word *humble* caught in Nia's chest like a breath she couldn't exhale. Humble didn't feel right. Nothing about standing in another woman's shadow felt like humility. It felt like fear dressed up as reverence.

She followed Tasha down the narrow stairwell into the fellowship hall. The sound of rain muffled overhead, replaced by the hum of voices and the clinking of cups. The Rebuild Project Board had gathered around a long oak table, papers spread out between them like puzzle pieces.

Bishop Calloway sat at the head, flanked by two long-time ministry partners, Sister Denise and Elder Vaughn. Both married and both pillars of the old guard. Their eyes softened with sympathy when they saw Nia, but beneath the politeness she could sense the question they weren't asking aloud:

Can she really handle this?

Bishop Calloway rose as she approached. "Nia, child, thank you for coming. I know this is a heavy day."

She nodded. "Yes, sir."

He gestured to the seat beside him. "Your name's already on the charter. All that's left is a few confirmations, financial signatures, some program approvals, and we'll begin transitioning the leadership under your direction."

The words *your direction* rang strange in her ears.

She took the pen and stared at the first page. The line for "Executive Director" gleamed back at her, waiting. For a moment, she saw Laneshia's handwriting layered faintly over it, as if her spirit had signed it already. Nia's throat tightened. She thought of all the nights she'd sat across from that woman, listening, learning, being seen in ways she hadn't thought possible.

"Don't be afraid of becoming what God already saw in you..."

The pen trembled slightly in her hand, but she signed anyway.

When she looked up, everyone was watching. Sister Denise gave a small, polite clap, followed by the others.
"There it is," Bishop Calloway said with a smile that didn't quite reach his eyes. "The next chapter begins."

Nia tried to smile back, but her reflection in the glossy tabletop betrayed her. Her eyes looked lost and uncertain. The mirror again. A silent reminder that taking the seat didn't mean she had filled it.

The meeting dissolved into logistics. Budgets, outreach plans, upcoming events. Nia heard the words but absorbed none of them. Every now and then, a phrase drifted through: "funding request," "new women's fellowship," "community partnership." The kind of conversations she used to sit in on and take notes for. Now, they waited for her approval.

By the time it ended, the rain had started again.

Tasha caught up with her by the door. "You okay?"

"I will be," Nia said. "Eventually."

“You don’t have to be strong every second.”

“I’m not,” she said quietly. “I just don’t know what else to be.”

They walked into the parking lot, umbrellas tilted against the drizzle. The city smelled of wet pavement and magnolia trees. Traffic lights flickered in puddles, red and green reflections shifting like broken promises.

At the edge of the lot, Nia paused, looking back at the church one last time. In the reflection of a rain puddle, she could see the stained glass glowing faintly, the same dove caught mid-flight. Lightning flashed again, and for a heartbeat, it looked like the bird was moving.

The thunder followed. It was deep, rolling, and certain.
And for the first time since Laneshia’s passing, Nia whispered a prayer that wasn’t a plea.

“God... if You’re really in this, show me how to be her and still be me.”

The rain answered, soft and steady.

By Monday morning, the rain had thinned to mist, but the city still smelled like sorrow.
Atlanta’s skyline glimmered in soft gray, streaks of sunlight trying to find their way through retreating clouds. The streets steamed where the water met asphalt. Nia sat in her car, hands gripping the steering wheel, staring at the modest brick building that bore the painted words The Rebuild Project.

She had been here hundreds of times before. First as a volunteer, later as Laneshia's assistant, and eventually as her mentee. This morning felt different. The building seemed unfamiliar, heavier somehow, like grief had settled into the mortar.

Her phone buzzed. A text from Tasha:

You got this, boss lady. Don't let them rattle you.

Nia managed a smile, small but real.

Inside, the office was alive with Monday energy. Phones ringing, printers humming, and the faint gospel playing low from someone's speaker. The walls were covered in photos of community events, smiling faces, food drives, and youth programs. Every image carried Laneshia's shadow in the background, that unmistakable presence.

Now, all eyes turned to Nia.

A few staff members greeted her warmly. Some with genuine affection and others with politeness that felt practiced. She couldn't blame them. They were used to Laneshia's commanding presence, her charisma that filled a room before she even spoke. Nia was quieter, more introspective, a storm gathering instead of one already raging.

"Morning, Ms. Daniels," called Evelyn, the office administrator, a wiry woman in her fifties with kind eyes but a sharp tongue. "Got your meeting schedule ready. Board wants updates on the mentorship program. Oh and Sister Denise called. She's asking about the women's fellowship event this weekend."

"Already?" Nia murmured.

"She said Pastor Laneshia had promised to deliver the keynote." Evelyn hesitated. "Do you... want to take her place?"

The question hit harder than it should have.
"Let's talk about it later," Nia said softly. "I need to settle in first."

She closed herself in Laneshia's old office. A space that felt too big and too sacred at the same time. The faint smell of jasmine still lingered, woven into the curtains and the upholstery. On the desk sat a small wooden cross, a framed photo of Laneshia laughing with a group of young women, and a leather-bound journal marked *Vision Notes.*

Nia sat in the chair. The same chair Laneshia used to rock in during her late-night calls with pastors across the city. She ran her fingers along the desk's smooth edge, feeling the grooves where years of writing had worn the varnish thin. The chair creaked softly, as if still remembering its former occupant.

She should've felt inspired. Instead, she felt like an imposter sitting at a shrine.

"Okay, God," she whispered. "Here I am. Do what You're gonna do."

Her reflection stared back at her in the glass of a picture frame. Hair neatly pressed, makeup minimal, eyes tired but alive. There it was again. The mirror.
She didn't look like a leader.
She looked like a woman trying not to fall apart.

By noon, the office buzzed with preparation for the upcoming Women's Fellowship Conference. It had been one of Laneshia's signature outreach programs. An event that drew women from churches across Georgia. Nia remembered how Laneshia commanded those rooms: confident, warm, never apologizing for her presence.

Now, whispers were already circulating.

"Did you hear Nia's taking over the keynote?"
"Bless her heart, she's trying."
"She's sweet, but she ain't Laneshia."

The words reached her before the end of the day. They always did.

In ministry, gossip never traveled alone. It came hand-in-hand with *concern.*

That evening, after the last volunteer had gone home, Nia sat alone at her desk, the glow from the computer screen reflecting on the window beside her. Outside, clouds gathered again, dark and swollen.

Another storm.

Lightning flickered, and for a moment her reflection appeared in the glass. Her face superimposed over the city skyline. She looked strong. Capable. Almost like Laneshia. But when the thunder cracked. The image trembled and disappeared.

Her phone buzzed again. Another text.
This time, not from Tasha.
It was from an unknown number:

Heard you're stepping up, Ms. Daniels. The city's watching. Hope you're ready for the rain.

Nia's stomach tightened. She didn't recognize the number, but she didn't need to.
Atlanta was full of voices that wanted to test the ones who rose too soon.

She looked out at the gathering storm. The rain beginning to bead against the glass. Somewhere deep inside, grief and determination began to braid together into something harder...something like faith.

"Even storms make things grow," Laneshia had said.

"Then let it rain," Nia whispered.

The thunder answered her loud, rolling and sure.

The rain didn't stop that night. It fell in soft, steady rhythms that seemed to sync with Nia's heartbeat.

The office had emptied hours ago, but she remained. Seated behind Laneshia's desk just staring out at the wet blur of the city through the window. Streetlights shimmered across puddles like scattered candles. Like reflections dancing where her mind refused to rest.

She tried to pray, but the words kept dissolving before they reached her lips. All she could manage was silence. That strange language God sometimes spoke back in.

On the corner of the desk sat Laneshia's journal. The same leather-bound one Nia had seen so many times before, half-open during staff meetings, filled with

Scripture references, notes, sermon outlines, even little doodles in the margins. Nia hesitated before touching it. It felt too intimate, too sacred, to open.

But her fingers moved anyway.

Inside the cover, in that familiar looping handwriting, was a short note:

If you're reading this, it means my assignment here is finished. Don't let grief make you forget purpose. God chose you on purpose, for purpose.
Now, rebuild the ones who think they've broken too far to be loved.
— L.S.

Nia's throat closed around the words. She pressed the book to her chest, feeling the weight of both the message and the woman behind it.

She didn't know if she was ready. She only knew she couldn't turn back.

Thunder rippled again across the skyline, and the light flickered in the office. Her reflection shimmered briefly in the dark window, doubled, then fractured, and for an instant she saw both herself and Laneshia's faint image overlapped, the mentor and the student, the past and the future.

The storm outside howled. Inside, Nia whispered:

"Okay, God. I'm going to rebuild. Even if I have to start with myself."

She turned off the desk lamp, grabbed her coat, and stepped into the night. The rain greeted her like a baptism. It was cool, cleansing, and alive.

Each drop carried memory, loss, and the faintest spark of new beginnings.

And as she walked toward her car, she didn't notice the figure watching from across the street. There was a man leaning beneath a dark umbrella. His gaze following her with quiet curiosity.

He wasn't a stranger to The Rebuild Project.
But his story... and hers...hadn't yet begun.

“I used to think God rebuilt what was broken
back to how it was before.
Now I know He plants new things in the cracks —
things stronger, softer, and rooted in grace.
The breaking wasn’t the end.
It was the planting.”
— *Nia Daniels, The Rebuild Project*

"When God rebuilds you, He never uses the same blueprint.

You won't just recover — you'll resurrect."

"Even concrete can't stop a rose that's meant to bloom.

Some roots are written in heaven."

“What She Learned in the Quiet”

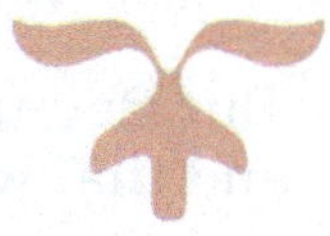

She didn’t rise all at once.
She rose in moments.
Small, trembling choices
to believe she was worth rebuilding.

In the quiet,
she learned that healing isn’t loud.
It doesn’t announce itself
or arrive with applause.
It comes softly,
like breath returning
to lungs that forgot how to trust the air.

She learned that letting go
is not losing,
and starting over
is not shame.
And sometimes the holiest thing
a woman can do
is choose herself
without asking permission.

People talked.
People wondered.
People misunderstood.

But God understood
and that was enough
to keep her moving.

She grew a little taller
in her truth.
A little softer
in her grace.
A little wiser
in her waiting.

And one day,
almost without noticing,
she looked back and realized:

The girl they doubted
had become the woman
she always needed.

The Weight of the Mantle

The mural of Laneshia Jonelle Stanson covered the eastern wall of The Rebuild Project's headquarters. A sweep of color and light that caught the dawn before the city woke. The artist had painted her smiling softly, eyes lifted toward a horizon of gold, one hand open as though releasing something invisible into the air. Nia Daniels stood beneath that painted gaze every morning before unlocking the front door.

It had been six months since the board had asked her to take over The Rebuild Project, six months since she'd promised to keep Laneshia's vision alive. And yet, standing there in the stillness of early morning, she felt a weight settle over her that had nothing to do with the cool Georgia air.

Responsibility, yes. But also, reverence.

Laneshia had been more than a mentor. She'd been a mirror, a compass, and sometimes a warning. Nia could still hear her voice: *"Don't mistake your purpose for your validation, baby. They're not the same thing."*

Nia exhaled, watching the breath leave her like a prayer. She was thirty-three, single, and by all outward measures, successful. The youngest director The Rebuild Project had ever appointed. A woman who had turned grief and faith into momentum. And yet, the quietest moments still pressed against her chest. Those moments when she wondered if she was enough, or if she was simply borrowing courage that hadn't been meant for her.

Inside the building, the scent of coffee lingered from yesterday's meeting. Files and flyers sat stacked neatly on the long conference table. Each one stamped with the new initiative she had designed: **Faith Forward: Women Reclaiming Ministry Spaces**.

That was her next fight. Opening the door for women like her to serve freely, without apology, without the quiet judgment that followed single women into every sanctuary.

But Nia knew that stepping back into the church would mean facing a different kind of scrutiny. She'd grown up in church halls that whispered about hips and hemlines. About who smiled too long or laughed too loud. And though she had spent years learning to love her plus-sized, curvy frame and learning that her body was not a battlefield, she also knew how easily it could be turned into one.

She brushed her palms over her navy dress, squared her shoulders, and whispered, “All right, Laneshia. I’ll do it my way.”

The sun crested the edge of the horizon then, washing the mural in soft gold. For a fleeting second, it felt like a benediction. A passing of the mantle from one woman’s faith to another’s fire.

Nia turned the key in the lock, pushed open the door, and stepped inside.

What she did not know yet, what no vision or mission statement could prepare her for, was that ministry would not just test her leadership. It would test her heart. Her faith. Her ability to forgive.

And somewhere, between board meetings and Sunday sermons, she would come to understand that misunderstanding could be its own kind of ministry. The place where grace learned to breathe.

1

The Return to Sanctuary

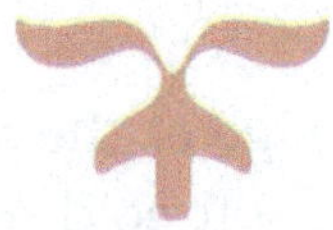

The first Sunday Nia Daniels returned to church, the Georgia air felt heavier than she remembered. That old kind of weight that pressed against both the skin and the spirit at once. It was the kind of heat that carried stories: old confessions, broken promises, and lingering prayers.

The morning sun slid slowly across the horizon. Even the wind seemed to hum low. Like it was still deciding whether to blow blessing or warning.

Greater Hope Tabernacle had changed since she'd last been there. The building wore its renovations like new Sunday clothes. Proud, but trying not to show off. The white steeple gleamed under the cloudless sky. Its gold cross catching the light so brightly that it made Nia squint. The once-faded siding had been painted a clean eggshell white. The cracked steps had been replaced with smooth stones. And out front, along the walkway, new rosebushes bloomed in clusters of soft pink and deep red roses that hadn't yet learned how to grow without thorns.

She parked beneath a magnolia tree whose heavy branches leaned towards her car like gossiping witnesses. The cicadas buzzed, persistent as memory, and somewhere nearby, a choir's rehearsal floated faintly through a cracked church window. Voices rising and falling in imperfect, beautiful harmony.

Nia turned off the ignition and sat for a moment, hands resting on the steering wheel. The faint hum of her engine faded into the heat. Her reflection in the rearview mirror looked composed. Lashes curled, lipstick understated, curls pulled back with quiet precision, but her heart was a small storm.

It had been nearly ten years since she'd set foot in a church like this. Ten years since she'd last worn heels that clicked against a sanctuary floor. Ten years since she'd decided that her faith could exist outside four walls.

She had once promised herself that she'd never walk through those doors again. That she'd pray from wherever she was. In her apartment, in the office, on the street and let that be enough.

But *The Rebuild Project*'s newest initiative, **Faith Forward**, changed that.

It was Laneshia's last vision before she passed. A citywide partnership with local churches to mend the gap between community work and spiritual renewal. And now it was Nia's job to lead it.

Returning to church wasn't just a task... it was obedience.

Laneshia had taught her that healing wasn't about avoidance. It was about *reclamation*.

"Sometimes," Laneshia had said, voice soft and steady as a hymn, "you go back not because you need them, but because somebody in there needs to see you come back."

That thought steadied her.

Still, her fingers trembled slightly as she gathered her purse and stepped out into the heat.

The air wrapped around her like fabric that was thick, humming, and alive.

When she reached the steps of Greater Hope, her heart skipped a beat. The doors stood open, wide and welcoming, but she knew better than to trust appearances.

Inside, the familiar scent of furniture polish and old wood hit her like memory. It mingled with perfume, aftershave, and the faint trace of peppermint that always seemed to float through Southern sanctuaries.

A young usher smiled nervously as she handed Nia a folded program.
"Welcome, ma'am. It's... it's good to see you."

Nia smiled back. "Thank you, baby."

The sound of the choir warming up washed through the sanctuary. That glorious, unfiltered hum that rose and fell like the tide of heaven meeting earth. Sopranos reaching for the edge of the sky, altos grounding them like roots.

For a moment, Nia closed her eyes and just listened. Music always had a way of untying her defenses.

"Nia Daniels?"

The voice came from her left. Warm, surprised, and edged with curiosity.

Turning, Nia saw Sister Alma Whitfield, the pastor's wife. Alma was slender, graceful, with a smile that never quite reached her eyes. Her pearls gleamed even in the low light.

"Lord, it's been years, hasn't it?" Alma said, her tone layered like Sunday cake, sweet on top, dense underneath. "I heard you're doing big things in the city. *The Rebuild Project*, right?"

Nia nodded, matching her pleasant tone. "Yes, ma'am. Just trying to continue what Laneshia started."

"Well," Alma said, resting a manicured hand on Nia's arm, "we were all *so proud* of her. Such a woman of... perseverance."

Nia caught the pause before that last word. The hesitation that dressed itself in grace but carried judgment just beneath.

It was the kind of word people used when they didn't want to say *scandal* or *rumor* out loud.

Still, she smiled, her voice steady. "Thank you. It means a lot to be here."

As she took her seat, she could feel it. That subtle shift. The invisible tightening of space around her that only women in ministry seemed to recognize.

It wasn't open hostility. It was something quieter, sharper.
A slight turning of shoulders. A sideways glance. A whispered name behind a fan.

Married women leaned subtly toward their husbands. A few eyes dipped toward her fitted cobalt-blue dress. One deacon's wife pursed her lips just enough for the gesture to sting.

Nia inhaled slowly. Deep and steady.

She knew this energy. She'd met it before. In other churches, in other pews. The unspoken question moving between them like air:

Why is she here now?

Her presence, her curves, her confidence. They filled the sanctuary differently. Not boastful. Not loud. But *seen.* And that alone was disruption enough.

When the service began, Pastor Whitfield stepped up to the pulpit. Tall and smooth-voiced. His rhythm, practiced. The sermon that morning was about *order in the house of God.*

His words rolled across the congregation like slow thunder, stirring polite amens and hallelujahs. But when his gaze met Nia's, something flickered in his expression. Recognition or maybe unease. Maybe it was curiosity he didn't know where to put.

She held his gaze for half a second longer than most would have, then looked away, unbothered.

After the benediction, the sanctuary turned into a slow-moving sea of handshakes and polite laughter. The sound of organ music filled the spaces where words hesitated.

Nia was gathering her purse when Sister Alma approached again. This time with two other women in tow.

Deaconess Brandy Cole and Minister Sandra Franks walked like pearls personified: smooth, deliberate, and practiced in posture. Their smiles glimmered without warmth.

"So good to have *new energy* in the house," Brandy said first, the kind of voice that smiled while measuring. "We could use some help with our women's fellowship. Maybe you could lead a workshop. You know, something about... *self-image*?"

Nia caught the subtext immediately. The glance toward her hips, the way Sandra's eyes flicked down her figure and then quickly back up with the performance of modesty.

"I'd love to," Nia replied, even and calm. "But maybe we start with something on *grace and leadership* first. You'd be surprised how often they go together."

Sandra's eyebrows rose. Alma laughed too quickly. "Well, I'm sure the pastor would appreciate that."

The three women exchanged looks, the kind of silent conversation that needed no words. Nia smiled through it. Standing a little taller. Her presence unshaken.

Later, driving home down Cascade Road, Nia replayed the entire interaction. Every smile. Every glance. Every coded word.

The old ache stirred. That subtle exclusion wrapped in Christian politeness. She'd felt it before. Years ago, when she'd led the youth ministry and found herself whispered about for wearing lipstick that was too red, or a dress that fit too right.

But she wasn't that woman anymore.

When she got home, she changed into soft cotton and sat at her writing desk, a hand-me-down from Laneshia. The wood still bore faint scratches from years of scribbled ideas and late-night prayers.

She opened her journal and let her pen do its thing. Another of Laneshia's habits she had kept.

Her pen moved slow, deliberate:

They misunderstand confidence for arrogance.
Curves for temptation.
Purpose for pride.

But I know who I am.
And I know Who sent me.

She paused, her eyes wet but steady.

Then she closed the notebook, lit a lavender candle, and whispered a quiet prayer. Not for approval, but for endurance.

"Lord," she murmured, "let them see You before they see me. And if they can't, help me stand anyway."

The flame flickered. Outside, thunder rolled far off in the distance, soft but steady, like a reminder that storms weren't always curses. Sometimes, they were the sound of heaven rearranging the air.

Greater Hope Tabernacle might not have been ready for her return, but she was ready to show them what a redeemed woman looked like when she stopped apologizing for her calling.

And when she laid her pen down, a faint smile tugged at her lips.
Laneshia's voice echoed softly in her spirit:

"Reclaim it, baby. Even the parts they tried to shame you for."

2

Women's Fellowship

The fellowship hall smelled like lemon oil and devotion. The kind of clean that wasn't just physical. It was spiritual. The sort of cleanliness that said someone had prayed while they mopped. The folding chairs had been arranged in a neat semi-circle, the kind that looked inviting but always left just enough space for distance. Not quite intimacy but also not quite isolation.

Sunlight streamed through the high basement windows, casting gold rectangles across the waxed tile floor. The hum of the air conditioner fought against Georgia's late-summer humidity, losing slightly, but trying valiantly.

At the back of the room, a long table held pitchers of sweet tea sweating into puddles, Styrofoam cups stacked in small towers, and trays of butter cookies shaped like flowers. The kind that left crumbs of nostalgia and sugar on your fingertips. No one wanted to be the first to touch them. In church culture, that was a statement in itself. An unspoken courtesy that masked hierarchy.

It was Nia's first official workshop at Greater Hope Tabernacle.

Grace and Leadership: Women Walking in Purpose

She had printed the title on thick cream paper, framed it, and set it beside the podium like a promise. Every detail mattered to her. Not for appearance, but for intention. Laneshia had taught her that presentation was ministry too.

Fifteen women came that Saturday morning. Some young and bright-eyed, others seasoned and steady. Most were dressed in shades of lavender and pearl, the unofficial uniform of church womanhood. It's where color means unity, but sometimes, also means conformity. Their Bibles sat open on their laps, pages softened from years of use.

They carried a mix of curiosity, quiet scrutiny, and that guarded kind of grace that came from women who had learned to protect their peace.

At the back of the room sat Reverend Caleb Morris, the new associate pastor. He had joined Greater Hope two months earlier. A widower, mid-forties, with a calm demeanor and the kind of presence that drew attention without demanding it. His voice was steady and deep. The sort that could silence a room without raising in volume.

He wasn't on the schedule for the workshop, but when he arrived that morning and saw the flyer, he'd told Alma he was "just there to support."

Nia had smiled when she saw him take a seat, notebook in hand. Men didn't usually show up to women's ministry events unless they were speaking or supervising. But he'd come quietly, without agenda. That was rare.

She adjusted her microphone and took a breath.

"Let's start," she said, her tone warm but assured, "by defining grace. Not the kind we say before dinner, but the kind that steadies us when we're misunderstood."

Her voice carried gently, but with authority.

The room shifted. A few women leaned forward. Others folded their arms politely, but measured. Nia recognized that posture. It was the one women used when they weren't sure whether to trust what they were hearing or who was saying it.

"Grace," she continued, pacing slowly before them, "is not permission. It's *positioning.* It's how God keeps us in purpose even when people think we don't belong in the room."

A murmur of agreement rippled through the chairs.

Nia smiled, encouraged. Her words weren't rehearsed. They came from the marrow of lived experience.

From the corner, Sister Alma Whitfield's lips pursed. Her posture perfect, her expression neutral. But the way her head tilted slightly to the side told Nia everything.

When the discussion opened, Minister Sandra Franks spoke first. Her tone sweet but lined with something sharper. "It's true, Sister Nia," she said brightly. "But sometimes we bring misunderstandings on ourselves. The Bible says to avoid even the *appearance* of impropriety."

There it was. The coded message wrapped in Scripture. The soft-spoken rebuke disguised as counsel.

Nia smiled, unshaken. "Yes, ma'am, it does. But it also says that *man looks at the outward appearance, while God looks at the heart.*" She paused, letting the silence stretch just long enough. "We all appear as something to somebody. That's why grace is necessary."

The room reacted in a few smothered chuckles, one soft "Amen," and a wave of relief from the younger women in the back who had been holding their breath.

Even Reverend Morris smiled, one brow lifted, his eyes glinting with quiet admiration.

The tension loosened.

As the session went on, Nia moved through her outline, but her words came alive with testimony. She talked about leadership not as dominance but as service. About grace not as weakness but as divine restraint. Her authenticity disarmed them.

One by one, the women began to speak. Hesitant at first, then open. Stories poured out like long-held confessions. A deaconess struggling in a silent marriage. A young ministry assistant afraid her calling made her unlikable, and even an older woman confessing how she'd lost her sense of purpose after years of serving without thanks.

Nia listened to each of them. Not as a leader, but as a sister.

She asked questions that made them think, not defend. She reminded them that God's call wasn't canceled by people's opinions. She quoted Laneshia once, softly:

"You can't build the Kingdom with broken identity. Healing *is* leadership."

By the end, the air felt lighter. A kind of holy release that always followed truth spoken in love.

When the last woman left, the fellowship hall echoed with the faint hum of the air conditioner and the distant clatter of someone washing dishes in the kitchen.

Sister Alma lingered by the doorway, her perfume hanging in the air like an afterthought.

"You certainly know how to hold a room," she said.

"I just tell the truth," Nia replied, stacking her notes.

Alma's smile was delicate, but her eyes flickered. "Truth can be... *disruptive.*"

"Sometimes it needs to be," Nia said, meeting her gaze without flinching.

Across the room, Reverend Morris pretended to busy himself stacking chairs, but Nia caught the small grin tugging at the corner of his mouth.

When Alma finally left, the room felt a few degrees cooler.

Caleb crossed the floor toward her. His steps easy...unhurried. Up close, she noticed the faint silver at his temples and the warm scent of cedar that clung to his suit.

"You handled that with grace," he said, resting a folded chair against the wall. "And precision."

She smiled, brushing an invisible wrinkle from her dress. "Thank you, Reverend. I'm learning those two things must work together."

He chuckled. A quiet, genuine sound. "You remind me of something my wife used to say. Grace without truth is sentiment, but truth without grace is cruelty."

Nia's expression softened. "Then I guess we're both still trying to find that balance."

There was a pause. Gentle and unforced. The kind that let silence do its own kind of talking.

For a fleeting moment, the fluorescent lights seemed softer, the space between them charged but not uncomfortable.

They spoke for a few minutes longer — about leadership, community, and The Rebuild Project's plans to mentor young women in ministry. But beneath the professional exchange was something else — an ease that neither flirtation nor formality could explain.

It felt... familiar. Peaceful.

When Nia finally gathered her things, Caleb held the door open for her.

"See you tomorrow, Sister Daniels," he said, his tone light but his eyes holding hers a second longer than necessary.

"See you tomorrow, Reverend."

Driving home that afternoon, windows down, the warm breeze tangling her curls, Nia found herself replaying the conversation.

She didn't call it chemistry. Not yet. That word carried too much history. She called it familiar peace. The quiet recognition between two souls who understood the same kind of solitude.

At a stoplight, she whispered a line Laneshia used to repeat whenever something stirred the spirit unexpectedly:

"Not every open door is meant to be walked through. But some are meant to remind you that you're still invited."

That night, she opened her journal, her favorite pen gliding across the page.

Grace can open doors.
But discernment keeps you from walking through the wrong ones.

She closed the book, exhaled, and leaned back in her chair. Outside, the sound of crickets filled the night.

Atlanta pulsed quietly around her. City lights flickering like prayers waiting for answers.

For the first time in a long time, Nia felt not just called, but seen.

3

Unholy Alliances

The following Sunday, the sun rose slow over Atlanta, laying streaks of amber across the skyline like God was sketching the city in gold before letting it live again.

Nia pulled into the church parking lot an hour early, the soft hum of gospel spilling from her car speakers. She cut the ignition and sat still, both palms resting on the steering wheel. Her breath fogged the glass for a moment before fading.

She'd promised herself not to let distraction steal her peace. She was here to serve. Not to be swayed...not to be shaken.

But determination didn't silence noise and Greater Hope Tabernacle had been buzzing all week.

By midweek, she'd already heard the whispers:

"That Rebuild lady think she somebody."
"She's too friendly with the Reverend."
"She's trying to change too much, too fast."

The first time she heard it, she laughed. A dry, knowing laugh that never quite reached her eyes. Not because it was funny, but because she recognized the rhythm of it.

Churches were families, and families didn't always know how to handle growth. They said they wanted revival, but not if it meant rearranging their comfort.

Still, by the third repetition, it stung.

Even the strongest woman can only armor herself so much before words find their way in.

She took a deep breath, then another, pressing her hand to her chest. "Focus," she whispered.

Today, Reverend Caleb had invited her to speak briefly before his sermon and give a short presentation about **Faith Forward**. This was the newest initiative from The Rebuild Project.

"Just a few minutes," he'd said when he called earlier that week. "Our people need to see what God's doing outside these four walls."

It wasn't lost on her that he'd said *our people.* Not *my* congregation, but *our.* That choice of words meant something.

Inside, the sanctuary was cool and softly lit, the smell of furniture polish and lilies mingling in the air. The choir rehearsed quietly up front. Humming the chords of "Total Praise," their harmonies like sunlight breaking through glass.

When she stepped onto the platform, time seemed to still for a breath.

Nia wore a tailored emerald dress that caught the light each time she moved. Not flashy, just confident. It matched the calm in her spirit, though her heart was anything but calm.

Her message was simple: restoration, inclusion, and the courage to rebuild.

She spoke about second chances. Not just for buildings or programs, but for people who'd lost faith in faith itself. Her voice carried a steady, melodic tone. The kind that filled the room without strain.

As she spoke, she caught sight of faces across the pews. Curiosity in some, caution in others. But she also saw hunger. Real hunger. The kind that recognized truth when it heard it, even if it didn't know how to receive it yet.

When she finished, there was that half-second pause before polite applause. The breath between agreement and hesitation. It didn't matter. The Word had landed where it needed to.

After service, she was gathering her notes when a small group of younger women approached her with bright smiles and hopeful eyes.

"Sister Nia, that was powerful," one of them said. "We've been praying about doing something like that for our age group."

Another added shyly, "Can we volunteer with The Rebuild Project? Maybe help with Faith Forward?"

Their energy warmed her. She took their names, offered hugs, and spoke encouragement into their hands. Moments like these! This was why she came back.

But peace never lingered long without challenge.

As she stepped outside into the warm afternoon, she spotted Deaconess Brandy Cole and Sister Alma Whitfield near the parking lot. Heads close together. Voices hushed but urgent. When they saw her, conversation snapped shut like a door caught mid-slam.

Nia smiled anyway. "Morning," she said, her tone even, gracious.

"Morning," Alma replied. Her smile was poised, her voice dipped in sugar. "Good message. *Bold.*"

"Thank you," Nia said lightly.

Brandy tilted her head. "You and Reverend Morris seem to make a good team."

The way she said *team* carried the sweetness of honey and the sting of a bee.

Nia held her composure, pausing long enough to make the silence hers. "The goal is the same. To build people, not platforms."

Alma tilted her head slightly, eyes narrowing just enough to draw meaning. "Just be careful, dear," she said softly. "Folks might... *misunderstand* your intentions."

There it was again. That word. The word that had followed her since she was called to ministry.

Misunderstood.

The label that let people judge you without admitting they feared you.

She smiled. It was slow, measured, and unconcerned. "They usually do," she said, and turned to leave before the silence could swallow her.

That afternoon, as sunlight faded across her living room wall, her phone rang.

"Reverend Caleb Morris," the caller ID read.

She hesitated before answering. Not because she didn't want to, but because she wanted to steady her tone.

"Hey, Reverend," she said when she picked up.

"I heard some chatter," he said gently, his voice calm but carrying weight. "You doing all right?"

"I'm fine," Nia said, though the fatigue in her voice betrayed her. "Comes with the territory."

"I know," he replied. "The higher you go, the thinner the air and the louder the echoes."

That line made her smile despite herself. "You've got a way with words."

"Preacher's curse," he said with a laugh. Then, more softly, "Don't let it distract you. You're doing good work."

They talked for a while about strategy, about mentorship, and about The Rebuild Project's upcoming community outreach. Somewhere in the conversation, he mentioned his late wife, Denise, and how she'd once been criticized for teaching the Word too confidently.

"She used to say the same thing you did," he said. "'People confuse conviction with arrogance.'"

Nia's voice softened. "Then she must've been strong."

"She was," he said quietly. "And lonely sometimes for it."

Silence hung between them. Not uncomfortable, but weighted with understanding.

They ended the call cordially, with a quiet blessing. Yet when Nia set her phone down, she found herself staring at it longer than she meant to.

There was something in his tone. Not flirtation nor pity. Just... presence.

The kind of presence that steadied, not stirred.

That evening, she sat on her porch, the city's hum stretching into twilight. The sky over Atlanta burned tangerine and violet, the skyline a jagged silhouette against the glow.

She thought of Laneshia. Of how she had carried her ministry through rumor, through betrayal, through loss, and still radiated grace that disarmed her critics.

In that memory, Nia found comfort.

“Lord,” she whispered into the warm air, “help me walk this road without bitterness. Help me stay soft in a world that rewards hard hearts.”

A breeze lifted her curls and brushed her cheek like an answer.

The next day, she stood before the board of The Rebuild Project. The conference table gleamed under fluorescent light, the air heavy with polite formality.

Word of the church murmurs had somehow reached them too.

“Some of us think,” said Mrs. Hanley, the chairwoman, tapping her pen, “that perhaps you should scale back your church involvement. We wouldn’t want anything... distracting from your leadership here.”

Nia folded her hands calmly. Her gaze steady, her voice even.

“With all respect,” she began, “our mission is to rebuild faith where it’s fractured. How can I teach restoration if I’m afraid to stand in the rubble?”

The room fell silent.

For a long moment, no one moved. Then Mrs. Hanley's pen stilled, and she gave a reluctant nod. "Point taken."

Meeting adjourned.

Nia gathered her folders and walked out with her head high, though her heart felt heavy. She could feel the tension tightening around her. Small, yet strategic. Spiritual.

The tests were coming faster now.

But so was her confidence.

That night, she sat by the window of her bedroom, city lights glittering like distant candles, and opened her journal.

Her handwriting was steadier than her heart.

Every misunderstanding is an invitation to clarify, not collapse.

She closed the book, whispering the words again like a prayer.

And somewhere in the quiet, in the soft hum of the city and the faint rustle of trees, she imagined Laneshia's mural smile widening just a little. As if heaven itself approved.

4

The Pastor's Wife's Table

The invitation came on a Monday morning, tucked neatly under Nia's office door at The Rebuild Project. The first thing she noticed was the paper. It was thick, cream cardstock. Expensive to the touch and the gold-embossed lettering that shimmered in the morning light:

You are cordially invited to the Greater Hope Women in Leadership Luncheon hosted by First Lady Alma Whitfield.

It was formal. Elegant. And unmistakably strategic.

There was no handwritten note, no personal greeting, not even a signature. Just her name, typed in perfect calligraphy.

For a long moment, Nia turned it over in her hands, the paper whispering faintly as it caught between her fingers. The gesture was deliberate. Too polished to be spontaneous and too pristine to be warm.

An olive branch? Or a test?

By Saturday, she'd decided it didn't matter.

Whatever the reason, she would show up. Not as a statement, but as herself.

The morning of the luncheon broke humid and bright. Nia stood before her mirror, fastening the delicate clasp of a gold bracelet. Her reflection was calm and thoughtful. She had chosen a soft blush wrap dress that fell just below the knee. It was modest, feminine and quietly confident. The fabric gathered gently at her waist, flowing as she moved.

Her jewelry was understated. Small gold hoops, a single ring, and the bracelet she now adjusted. Her hair, a crown of natural curls that framed her face like a halo of resilience.

She didn't dress to impress. She dressed to belong. And belonging, in spaces built to exclude her, had always been her most radical act.

As she drove toward the Whitfield's neighborhood, the roads grew wider and the houses became larger. Manicured lawns gave way to wrought-iron gates and flowerbeds designed to look effortless. The Whitfield's home sat at the curve of the cul-de-sac. It was a stately brick house with white columns and wide steps. It was the kind of place where prayer meetings and political strategy shared the same table.

A valet directed cars up the circular drive. BMWs, Lexuses, and a black Escalade gleaming like authority itself.

Inside, the scent of cinnamon and vanilla filled the air, layered over polished mahogany and the faint trace of floral air freshener. Laughter floated from the dining room. Soft. Rehearsed with that particular pitch that women used to perform grace under scrutiny.

“Welcome, Sister Daniels!”

Alma appeared in the foyer, radiant in a cream suit that looked hand-tailored, her pearls perfectly placed, her smile balanced between warmth and hierarchy.

“So glad you could make it,” she said, voice honeyed.

“Thank you for inviting me,” Nia replied, extending a small gift bag of handmade candles. The label read *Light & Grace*, from a local women’s collective she often supported. It was a peace offering. Or at least a declaration of peaceful intent.

“Oh, how thoughtful.” Alma took the bag, her manicured fingers brushing Nia’s lightly before she passed it to a waiting assistant. “Come on in. The others are in the dining room.”

The table gleamed under a chandelier that looked like it could hold prayers and secrets equally well. Twelve seats, each with gold-rimmed plates and folded linen napkins shaped like lilies.

The women were already seated in their subtle order. Alma at the head, naturally, with her closest allies on either side. To Nia's left sat Minister Sandra Franks, all pearls and precision. A woman who never blinked without meaning it. To her right was a newcomer, Sister Rochelle Hayes. She was young and newly married. Still glowing with the fragile confidence of early ministry.

Across the table, the women chatted about choir programs, conference budgets, and who would host the next prayer breakfast. Their voices rose and fell like a choir. Harmonized but not entirely sincere.

Beneath the sound, Nia could feel the undercurrent. Glances that lingered just a heartbeat too long and laughter that sometimes sharpened at the edges.

Alma clinked her spoon against her glass. "Before we eat, I'd like to thank everyone for their service," she began, her voice smooth, practiced. "The women of Greater Hope have always been the backbone of this church. And now, with Sister Nia leading new initiatives in the community, I believe we're entering a season of... expansion."

Polite applause followed. Gentle, measured, and obligatory.

Nia smiled, offering a small nod. "I'm grateful for the opportunity to serve," she said softly.

Alma tilted her head, tone light. "Tell us more about your project," she said. "Faith Forward, isn't it?"

"Yes," Nia said, meeting her gaze evenly. "It's about empowering women in ministry. Giving them tools to lead with confidence and compassion, inside and outside the church."

Brandy Cole, seated two chairs down, leaned forward. "So, it's just for single women?"

The question hung in the air like perfume. Sweet but suffocating.

"No," Nia replied evenly, her voice smooth as satin. "It's for called women. Married, single, or widowed. Whoever God uses."

A few forks paused midair.

Alma's lips curved. "That's beautiful. Of course, we must also remember that a woman's strength should complement her covering, not compete with it."

The table murmured approval, heads nodding like metronomes of respectability.

From the far end, Nia heard a quiet mention of Reverend Caleb's name in passing. Something light…teasing. The bait.

She took a slow sip of water before responding. "I agree, First Lady. But every woman has a covering. God Himself. Sometimes that has to be enough."

The silence that followed was not hostile but it was just… charged.

The chandelier's crystals seemed to tremble faintly in the still air.

Sandra cleared her throat. "Still, Sister Nia," she began, voice taut with propriety, "appearances matter. You're a beautiful woman. People notice things. And in ministry, that can be... distracting."

Nia's smile didn't waver. Her tone remained soft, but her words carried weight. "Then maybe it's time we stop teaching women to shrink so others can stay focused. Maybe the issue isn't appearance, but perception."

This time, no one spoke.

Even Alma's practiced smile faltered, just slightly — enough for anyone paying attention to see the crack.

And it was Rochelle, the youngest at the table, who broke the tension.

"I needed to hear that," she said quietly. "Sometimes I feel like I'm too much for this space. Like I have to apologize for wanting to lead."

Nia turned toward her, her voice gentle but firm. "Don't you ever apologize for light. Just learn how to carry it without burning yourself."

Something shifted.

The atmosphere, once taut with silent judgment, began to ease. Not entirely, but noticeably. The air softened.

For the rest of the luncheon, conversation flowed differently. Less performance, more presence. Even laughter sounded real this time. Not rehearsed or strained. Genuine.

Nia hadn't just entered their circle; she had rearranged its center.

When dessert came, peach cobbler with ice cream, melting lazily against the warm crust, Alma rose to make her closing remarks.

"Well, this has been lovely," she said, voice even but her eyes a shade sharper than before. "Sister Nia, you certainly have a way with words."

"Thank you," Nia replied. "Words are seeds. I just hope they fall on good soil."

Alma's eyes glimmered, her voice velvet. "We'll see what grows."

Later that evening, Nia sat on her porch, the air thick with the hum of summer. Lightning bugs flickered like tiny prophecies in the dark.

She thought of Alma. The way power could hide behind grace. How jealousy could dress itself up as discernment. But she also thought of Rochelle, and how one woman's courage could water another's roots.

She opened her journal, pen in hand.

At some tables, you're not invited to eat. You're invited to prove you belong. But grace doesn't need permission to sit down.

She underlined the last sentence twice.

Across town, Reverend Caleb sat in his office at the church, a single lamp burning beside his desk. He was reviewing Nia's proposal for the next *Faith Forward* conference.

Her words pulled at him. Not romantically, but spiritually. The kind of pull that reminded him of why he still believed in his calling. Even after loss.

He read her closing line again:

Rebuilding faith requires dismantling fear.

He smiled faintly and leaned back in his chair.

He didn't know why her words stayed with him long after he set the paper aside. Only that they did.

And in some small, sacred place of his heart, he whispered a prayer neither of them would yet understand:

"Lord, protect her calling. She's walking through fire wearing peace like linen."

5

Rumors and Reverence

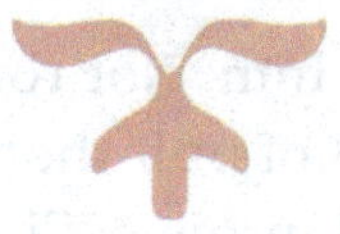

The Sunday after the luncheon, the sanctuary air was thick with perfume, humidity, and speculation. Whispers traveled faster than the choir's harmonies. You could almost see them. Invisible threads winding between pews and slipping into the corners of conversation.

Nia had expected some fallout. She just hadn't expected it to spread this fast.

Her workshop notes had barely cooled on her desk before someone decided she was "getting too comfortable with leadership." By midweek, a story had surfaced that she and Reverend Caleb Morris were "spending late nights planning programs." Another said they'd been seen "laughing too long" after a meeting.

It would have been laughable if it hadn't been so familiar.

Laneshia had once told her, *"A woman in ministry is either invisible or infamous. You decide which one you can live with."*

Nia chose neither. She chose integrity. But integrity didn't always translate well in circles that thrived on speculation.

That Sunday morning, she wore navy blue. A color that made her feel grounded. She took her seat near the front, aware of the eyes following her. Reverend Morris stood at the pulpit, his sermon on *The Weight of Words*. His voice rolled low and steady through the sanctuary, deliberate as a drumbeat.

"Sometimes," he said, "we confuse discernment with gossip. One comes from the Spirit; the other from insecurity."

Nia felt the air still. The timing wasn't lost on anyone.

His gaze drifted briefly toward her. Not in defense, but in acknowledgment. The kind that said, *I see you standing through it.*

When service ended, she gathered her bag quickly. Outside, several of the younger women caught her arm. "Sister Nia, we heard what people saying. It ain't right," said one.

"It's fine," she replied gently. "Let them talk. Truth has a longer lifespan."

She smiled, but her chest ached with the quiet exhaustion that came from always having to prove purity in a world obsessed with suspicion.

By Tuesday, she was summoned to meet with the church board. The letter was polite, but the phrasing, *"for clarity and accountability"*, hinted at interrogation more than inquiry.

When she entered the conference room, the walls felt closer than usual. Pastor Whitfield sat at the head of the table, his wife to his right, the elders fanning out like a jury. Reverend Morris sat to the side, hands folded, expression unreadable.

"Nia," Pastor Whitfield began, voice pastoral but clipped, "we've been hearing some concerns from members about appearances. You and Reverend Morris have been working closely. We just want to ensure everything remains above reproach."

Nia inhaled slowly, then nodded. "Understood, Pastor. Every meeting we've had has been professional. Most have been in public spaces. Church offices, Rebuild headquarters, or planning sessions."

Alma leaned forward, voice syrupy-smooth. "Of course, dear. But you must understand how people perceive things. A woman of your... *presence* attracts attention."

Nia met her gaze calmly. "Respectfully, First Lady, perception is the responsibility of the perceiver."

A faint murmur moved through the room.

Pastor Whitfield cleared his throat. “Let’s all remember why we’re here. To preserve integrity in ministry.”

Reverend Morris finally spoke. “And to preserve dignity, sir. Sister Nia has conducted herself with nothing but professionalism. If people are uncomfortable with collaboration between a man and a woman, perhaps we should question that discomfort instead of her integrity.”

For the first time, Alma’s composure cracked, just slightly.

Pastor Whitfield shifted. “Let’s... move forward in unity,” he said, ending the meeting before the conversation could dig deeper.

As Nia stood to leave, he added, “Sister Nia, you’re doing good work. But a wise woman once told me that fire draws eyes, and not everyone watching wants you to shine.”

She smiled faintly. “Then maybe I’ll build something that can withstand the heat.”

By Thursday, the whispers had turned into silences. The kind that followed her into rooms and echoed louder than words ever could. She caught the sideways glances, the quick hush when she entered the fellowship hall.

But there were other voices too. Softer, truer ones.

Rochelle texted her that morning: *"Keep doing what you're doing. Some of us need to see it done right."*

That same evening, she found a note slipped under her office door at The Rebuild Project. The handwriting was elegant, unmistakably Caleb's:

"The rumors will fade, but the fruit will remain. Keep your focus. You're not fighting for your name, you're fighting for theirs."

She folded the note and placed it inside her journal, right beside Laneshia's favorite quote: *"Grace never loses its grip, even when your reputation does."*

Later that night, she sat at her kitchen table with a cup of peppermint tea, heavy exhaustion in her shoulders. She thought about how easily women's worth could be rewritten by rumor. How a single whisper could drown out a thousand prayers.

Still, she prayed anyway.

"Lord, make me steady when I'm shaken. Let me remember who called me, even when the crowd gets loud."

By Sunday, something shifted.

The very same women who had whispered began to approach her quietly after service. Not to apologize, but to align. They saw how she hadn't flinched, how she kept showing up with grace and professionalism, no bitterness, no defensiveness.

In the strange economy of church politics, resilience had currency.

Rochelle hugged her in the hallway. “They’re starting to respect you now,” she whispered.

Nia smiled softly. “Respect earned through endurance always lasts longer than the kind given out of pity.”

And then, as if by divine irony, Pastor Whitfield announced from the pulpit that next month’s Women’s Revival would be led by none other than *Sister Nia Daniels*, “A woman whose faith and fortitude exemplify what this church stands for.”

Alma’s smile from the front pew was polished porcelain.

Reverend Morris clapped with quiet pride, his eyes meeting hers only briefly.

And in that instant, Nia felt something rise inside her. Not triumph, but peace.

Because she finally understood. Rumor couldn’t undo revelation.

That night, she wrote her longest journal entry yet:

“They can misunderstand your motives, your tone, even your calling. But they can’t undo what God has already assigned to your name. Reverence isn’t just worship. It’s how you carry yourself when the world is watching to see if you’ll break.”

She closed her notebook, whispered a soft amen, and let the peace of it settle into her bones.

Outside, the cicadas sang their endless song. Low and steady. Unbothered by the noise of the world.

And somewhere deep in her spirit, she felt Laneshia smiling again.

6

The Revival

The announcement had settled into the congregation like a summer storm. Thrilling to some but unsettling to others.
Sister Nia Daniels, first-time keynote for the Women's Revival.
The murmurs were almost audible as she walked down the hall the following Sunday. Some congratulatory, others cloaked in surprise. And a few, from the pews of the First Ladies' Ministry Circle, were downright skeptical.

It was one thing to lead workshops. Quite another to hold the microphone when the sanctuary was full. The air expectant. The audience filled with women who had built their lives around hierarchy and decorum.
But the thought didn't frighten Nia. Not anymore.

Because she'd been through worse battles. Silent ones fought in dark rooms. Unspoken wars against rumor and insecurity. And she'd survived them all.

Still, the revival loomed in her mind like a mountain she hadn't yet climbed.

Two weeks before the revival, Nia sat in her apartment surrounded by index cards, notebooks, and the gentle hum of her air conditioner. On the table lay her sermon outline: *"The Rebuild Within: Becoming the Woman God Intended Before the World Told You Who to Be."*

She'd rewritten it six times. Each draft, sharper, more honest than the last.

Laneshia had always said, *"The best sermons are lived before they're preached."* And if that was true, Nia had been preaching this one her whole life.

Her phone buzzed.

Caleb Morris: *Working late on your outline again? Don't forget to breathe.*

She smiled. His texts had become a quiet rhythm in her life. Gentle nudges that felt both pastoral and personal.
Nia: *Trying to make sure I don't say something that gets me escorted out by the ushers.*
Caleb: *If they escort you out, I'll walk with you. Some truths are worth the exit.*

She stared at the screen for a long moment, the corners of her mouth curving despite herself. His words held a weight that went beyond charm. They carried recognition. The understanding of a woman who had been misjudged but still chose to serve.

And though they had never crossed lines, never spoken words they shouldn't, the energy between them hummed like electricity under quiet restraint.

In the days leading up to the revival, the tension in the church office could have been bottled and sold.

Alma and her circle of married ministry wives, elegant, composed, and perpetually accessorized, began holding "special prayer sessions" in the parlor. They prayed loudly, with pointed phrases that landed like darts wrapped in scripture.

"Lord, keep our young women focused on ministry, not on men's attention."
"Lord, let our sisters know that beauty is not a calling."

Nia passed by once and caught the tail end of a comment that froze her in place.
"...some women use the Word to get a man's gaze, not his soul."

She didn't need to guess who "some women" were.

Later, she sat in her car, hands gripping the steering wheel. For a moment, she wanted to scream. Not because the words hurt, though they did. but because she was tired.

Tired of being reduced to body and beauty before heart and calling.

She pulled out her phone and scrolled to her notes app, typing a line she'd use later in her message: *"There will always be people who mistake confidence for pride, and presence for temptation. But that's their insecurity, not your sin."*

The Night Before...

The sanctuary was empty except for Nia and the janitor, who hummed softly as he swept the aisles. The revival banner hung proudly across the stage:

"Women Rebuilt: Restored, Resilient, Redeemed."

Nia stood at the pulpit, fingers resting on the smooth wood. The lights were dimmed, but even in the shadows, she could feel the weight of the space. The years of sermons, songs, and secrets soaked into the walls.

Her knees bent almost instinctively.
She prayed the way she had as a child, not for performance but for survival.

"Lord, don't let me speak to impress. Let me speak to heal. Let me be transparent enough that someone else can see through me to You."

As she rose, the back door creaked open. Caleb stepped inside, jacket draped over his arm. "Couldn't sleep?" he asked.

She smiled softly. "Didn't want to."

He walked closer, his voice low. "You ready?"

"As ready as I'll ever be."

He hesitated, then said quietly, "Don't let them shrink your voice to fit their comfort. You carry fire, Nia. Don't apologize for it."

For a moment, the air between them thickened. Not romantic, exactly, but intimate in the way two souls recognize each other's weight.

"Thank you," she whispered.

He nodded and left without another word, his footsteps echoing down the hallway like a benediction.

Saturday morning, the sanctuary was overflowing. Women in hats, heels, and expectancy filled every pew. The choir shimmered in gold robes, and the air was thick with perfume, body heat, and anticipation.

Alma opened the service with her usual polish. Her voice crisp and her smile fixed. But when she announced, “Our keynote speaker this morning, Sister Nia Daniels,” a visible ripple moved through the room. Some clapped eagerly. Others folded their arms.

Nia took the stage slowly. Her heart raced, but her steps were steady. She wasn’t the shy woman who once hid behind Laneshia’s shadow. She was a woman who had wrestled with God and found peace in the bruises.

Her message began softly. A story about rebuilding a life after rejection. About how The Rebuild Project was never just a job, but a calling born out of brokenness.

Then her tone shifted, rising with each line.

“Some of us were told that our worth ended when someone else stopped believing in us.
Some of us were made to feel like our stories were too messy for ministry.
But I came to tell you, God specializes in messy beginnings.”

Amens filled the air.

She looked across the sanctuary. There were women nodding, some wiping tears. Even Alma, though composed, couldn’t hide the flicker of discomfort in her eyes.

Nia continued, voice firm now.

“Don’t you dare shrink yourself to make insecure people comfortable.
Don’t you dare let someone tell you that your body is

a distraction.
God made you in full and if your presence intimidates, that's not your burden to carry."

The room erupted. A sea of applause, shouts, and tears.

For the first time, Nia felt the kind of authority that wasn't granted by men or permissioned by church tradition. It came from something higher. Something earned in the dark.

As the choir began to sing, she stepped back, heart pounding. Her eyes met Caleb's at the side of the stage. He didn't move, didn't smile. He just nodded once, reverently, as if to say: *You did it.*

When the sanctuary emptied, Alma approached her. For a heartbeat, Nia braced herself.

"You spoke... boldly," Alma said, her tone unreadable.

"Thank you," Nia replied.

Alma paused. "Some of us need time to adjust to new ways of speaking truth."

Nia smiled. "I understand. It took me years to learn to speak mine."

They stood in silence before Alma gave a tight nod and walked away.

Caleb appeared a moment later. "That," he said quietly, "wasn't just a sermon. It was a shift."

She exhaled. "It felt like one."

He hesitated, then added, "There's a men's leadership retreat next month. They're asking me to help organize it. I was thinking..." He trailed off. "Maybe you could speak there too. From a woman's perspective. Bridge the conversation."

Her brows rose. "You sure the board would approve that?"

He smiled faintly. "Let's just say I don't always ask permission to follow purpose."

Their laughter echoed softly through the hall.

And for the first time in a long time, Nia didn't feel misunderstood. She felt seen.

Not as a rumor. Not as a threat. But as a woman finally standing in the fullness of her calling.

That night, she wrote in her journal:

"Today I learned that reverence and revolution can live in the same heartbeat. I learned that grace can sound like thunder and still be holy. I learned that being misunderstood doesn't make me unworthy. It makes me human."

She set the pen down, leaned back, and smiled through her tears.

Outside, the night hummed quietly. Its sound was steady, patient...alive.

And Nia knew, this was only the beginning.

7

Bridges and Boundaries

The men's retreat was held two hours outside the city, tucked away in a quiet lakeside camp surrounded by tall pines and air that smelled like still water and new beginnings. It wasn't the kind of place Nia would have chosen for herself, but something about the remoteness felt right. Clean. Uncomplicated.

When Caleb first asked her to speak, she'd hesitated. The revival had been victory and notoriety enough. But something in his eyes, the conviction behind his tone, had made her pause before saying no.
He'd said, *"What if your voice is part of the healing they don't know they need?"*

Now, as she drove down the narrow dirt road leading to the retreat center, her nerves rose like static beneath her skin. She wasn't used to being the only woman in a room full of men of faith. Especially not after the whispers she'd endured.

But this invitation wasn't about comfort, it was about calling.

She parked her car and stepped out into the quiet. The lake shimmered like glass under the early afternoon sun. Birds called to each other across the water, and the low rumble of male laughter echoed from the dining hall up the hill.

Caleb met her halfway down the path, sleeves rolled up, clipboard in hand.
"You made it," he said, his grin easy, familiar.

"I almost turned around twice."

"I'm glad you didn't," he said. "We need your voice here."

She tried not to notice the way he looked. How the sunlight caught on the stubble along his jaw or how peace seemed to hang around him like a well-worn coat. He was ministry and man, both. Steady, careful, and watchful.
"You're the only woman," he said as they started walking toward the main lodge. "So prepare for awkward introductions."

She smiled. "Story of my life."

The Session

Her session was scheduled for that evening. The topic: *Bridging the Divide – Understanding the Women Who Serve Beside You.*

By the time she stood before the crowd, a hundred or so men seated in folding chairs, her palms were slick with sweat. But when she began to speak, the nerves melted away.

"I didn't come here to talk about women as mysteries," she said, voice calm but firm.
"I came to talk about women as ministers, leaders, and believers who've carried church pain in silence."

She saw the subtle shifts in the room. A combination of discomfort, curiosity, and conviction.

"Sometimes," she continued, "we ask women to build altars out of broken pieces and then fault them for bleeding on the bricks. We preach accountability but forget compassion."

A few heads bowed. A few men nodded.
And then she spoke about partnership. About how ministry should never be a competition between genders but a collaboration of callings.

When she finished, the room was still.
Then, slowly, applause rose.

Caleb stood in the back, watching her with an expression she couldn't quite read. Was it pride? Admiration? Or something else beneath it that she dared not name?

After dinner, the men gathered around campfires, their voices low and reflective. Nia sat alone on the deck overlooking the lake, a mug of tea warming her hands. The water reflected the stars like a field of light.

She didn't hear Caleb approach until he was beside her, leaning against the railing.

"You handled them better than I expected," he said.

She laughed softly. "You mean they didn't throw hymnals?"

He smiled. "I mean they listened. That's rarer than you think."

They stood in silence for a while. The night was thick with summer air and unspoken things.

"I've been thinking," he said finally, "about how easy it is to lose balance in ministry. To let calling become the thing that replaces connection."

She glanced at him. "You sound like a man speaking from experience."

"I am." His eyes stayed on the horizon. "I've spent years being the dependable one. The one who shows up, preaches, fixes, and leads but never lets anyone see him tired."

She nodded slowly. "And now?"

He exhaled, a faint smile touching his lips. "Now I'm realizing God never asked for perfection. Just presence. And some days, even that feels like faith."

She looked down into her cup, then back at him. "You ever get lonely?"

His gaze met hers, and for a heartbeat, something shifted in the air.

"All the time," he said quietly. "But I've learned to call it stillness."

Her breath caught. "That's a dangerous kind of peace."

"I know." He smiled again, softer this time. "But it's better than chaos."

Their eyes held a little longer than they should have. Long enough for both of them to remember the invisible line between purpose and longing.

Nia looked away first. "We should both get some rest," she said, voice steady but softer than before.

"Yeah," he said. "Before the stillness says too much."

The Next Morning....

The lake was mist-covered when she woke. Morning prayers echoed faintly from the open-air chapel across the camp. She slipped on her sweater and made her way down to the shore.

She found Caleb there, kneeling near the water's edge, Bible open on his lap.

He looked up when she approached but didn't speak.

She sat beside him, close enough to feel the warmth of his presence but not close enough to blur the line.

For a few moments, they just listened to the rippling water. To the chorus of morning birds and the sacred quiet between them.

Finally, he said, "Do you ever wonder if people like us… people who love deeply, serve fully… ever get to rest in love, too?"

She looked out across the water. "I think we do. But maybe not in the way the world expects. Maybe our kind of love is built on something slower. Something holy."

He nodded, his thumb tracing the worn edge of his Bible. "Holy doesn't mean easy."

"No," she whispered. "It means worth it."

He closed his eyes for a moment, as if sealing her words in prayer. Then he stood, brushing sand from his hands.

"We've got another session in an hour," he said gently. "You ready?"

She smiled. "Always."

When the retreat ended two days later, Nia stood by her car, saying goodbye to the men who had come to shake her hand and thank her for her message. Most spoke humbly, a few awkwardly, but every one of them looked changed somehow.

Caleb approached last, his expression unreadable.

"You changed the atmosphere here," he said.

"Not me," she replied. "Just truth finally given space to breathe."

He nodded, then added quietly, "Be careful when you go back. People notice when someone starts walking in peace. It stirs things up."

"I've already noticed," she said.

He smiled faintly. "I'll check in once we're both back in town. Maybe grab coffee. Church-approved and rumor-safe, of course."

"Of course," she said, though the laughter that followed carried something warmer, something unsaid.

As she drove away, she glanced once in the rearview mirror. Caleb still stood by the edge of the road, hands in his pockets, watching until her car disappeared around the bend.

And for a fleeting second, she allowed herself to feel what she would never name, that gentle ache of connection that didn't demand possession, just acknowledgment.

Because sometimes holiness didn't come from distance. It came from discipline.
And sometimes, restraint was its own kind of reverence.

That night, Nia wrote:

"There are bridges built not of wood or stone, but of trust. Fragile, sacred things suspended between what is and what could be. And sometimes, God lets two souls walk across one for just a moment. Not to join them, but to remind them they're not alone on the journey."

She closed her journal, the sound of the lake still echoing in her memory.

8

Fire and Silence

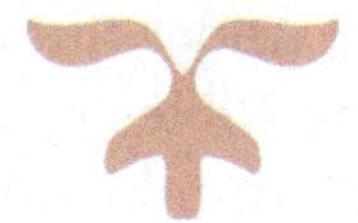

Sunday mornings had become both balm and battle. The Rebuild Project was thriving. There were more women enrolled than ever before, partnerships with churches across Atlanta, new donors, even whispers of expansion to other states. But success had brought visibility, and visibility had brought scrutiny.

The trouble began quietly, as trouble in church circles often did, in the women's fellowship meetings. At first, it was the glances. The way some of the married women would exchange looks when Nia entered the room, her soft curves framed in a modest but well-fitted dress. Then came the subtle remarks cloaked in laughter, "You know these single women stay dressed like they preaching for attention," or "She got a good heart, but she do too much for a single woman."
Each jab carried the sting of jealousy disguised as righteousness.

Nia ignored it at first. She had learned from Laneshia that not every battle deserved her peace. But quiet endurance has a shelf life, and when the whispers grew louder, she began to feel the weight of being misunderstood, again.

One Thursday afternoon, the ministry board gathered in the church conference room. They were seated at a long table under fluorescent light with cups of lukewarm and Bibles open like weapons. The discussion started about budgeting for The Rebuild Project's upcoming seminar. Nia presented her proposal confidently. It detailed expanding the mentorship program to include younger girls aging out of foster care.
Her words came from purpose, not ego. But purpose doesn't always protect you from politics.

Sister Marla, the pastor's wife and unofficial queen of decorum, adjusted her pearls before speaking.
"I appreciate your passion, Sister Daniels," she said, her tone coated with sweetness that didn't reach her eyes, "but some of us feel that this project is... well... becoming a bit too centered around you. The church is a body, not a brand."

The room fell into that uneasy silence where everyone is waiting to see which way the wind will blow.
Nia felt her pulse quicken. "It's not about me," she replied calmly. "It's about the women we're helping find their footing again. This is about transformation, not attention."

Marla smiled thinly. "Of course, dear. But transformation should happen within church walls, not on social media. You've been... quite visible lately. Some of our sisters are uncomfortable."

Uncomfortable. The word lingered like smoke.
Nia glanced around the table, searching for allies, but most of the women kept their eyes down. Even those who had once cheered her on now seemed content to fade into the wallpaper of caution.

Pastor Lyle finally cleared his throat. "Let's not let misunderstanding cause division. Sister Nia's work has been fruitful. But we must all guard our hearts and our witness."

That should have been the end of it. But Sister Marla wasn't finished.
"Guarding our hearts also means avoiding appearances that could bring temptation for ourselves or others," she added. Her gaze flicked briefly toward Reverend Caleb Morris, sitting two seats away.

And suddenly, every head turned.

The air went still. Nia's throat went dry. Caleb looked startled, then composed himself, shifting slightly in his chair. He was the one person in this church who had seen her beyond the labels. The first to volunteer at Rebuild workshops, the one who had prayed with her when she felt the weight of leadership crushing her chest. Their connection had always been innocent but real. An ease between them that others clearly did not understand.

Nia forced her voice to stay steady. “Are you implying something, Sister Marla?”
Marla tilted her head, lips pursed in mock humility. “Not at all. Just reminding our young leaders that boundaries protect blessings.”

The words sliced through the air like a knife.
A few people coughed. Someone whispered, “Lord, have mercy.”

Nia felt the room tilt, memories flashing of the times she had been misjudged, misunderstood, and silenced in the name of respectability. She could almost hear Laneshia’s voice in her mind: *You can’t control what people say, only how you carry truth inside you.*

But this, this cut deeper. Because it wasn’t just gossip. It was public humiliation.

Caleb’s hand twitched on the table. He looked at Marla and said quietly, “That’s unnecessary.”
Marla raised her brows. “Oh, is it? Then perhaps you can explain why the two of you were seen leaving together after Bible study last week.”

The room gasped in unison.
Nia opened her mouth to respond. To explain that they’d gone to pray with one of the young women who’d just lost her mother, that nothing inappropriate had ever happened, but before she could, the door opened.

Pastor Lyle’s wife, Sister Ruth, entered holding her phone, her face pale. “Pastor,” she said softly, “you need to see this.”

She turned the screen toward him.
His eyes widened.

A photo. Blurry, but clear enough to tell a story. Nia and Caleb standing outside the church in the dusk light, close, heads bowed together in prayer. But to an uncharitable eye, it looked like an embrace. Someone had taken the picture and posted it online with the caption: *This the kind of 'mentoring' they doing at The Rebuild Project now?*

The post had already gathered comments. Hundreds of them.

The room erupted.
Voices overlapped. Accusations, questions, murmurs of scandal.
Marla crossed her arms in triumph. "This is exactly what I meant. The devil works in appearances."
Caleb rose to his feet, his voice low but trembling. "That's a lie. We were praying for a grieving student. I won't sit here while you twist something sacred into gossip."

Nia stood too. "You will not turn my calling into controversy. I've worked too hard, prayed too long—"

"Sister Daniels," the pastor interrupted, his tone weary, "perhaps it's best if you step back from public ministry until this matter settles. For the good of the church."

The words struck like thunder.
Step back?! After everything?! After building Rebuild from ashes and turning judgment into healing?!

Nia stared at him, the walls of the conference room blurring.

"Are you asking me to stop serving because people are lying?" she whispered.

He didn't answer. That silence said everything.

Caleb started to speak, but Nia raised a trembling hand. "Don't," she said softly. "Not here."
She gathered her notebook, her heart pounding so hard she thought she might faint. Every eye in the room followed her as she walked to the door.

The hallway outside was quiet. Too quiet.
Her vision swam. Her breath came fast.
She stumbled into the stairwell, gripping the railing, tears slipping down her face. The city outside the stained-glass window glowed gold and red in the fading light, like fire caught in glass.

She pulled out her phone. A single message waiting from an unknown number:
You thought you could take my place. God don't bless mess.

Her chest tightened. Her hands shook.
She scrolled down and froze. The sender's profile photo was Sister Marla's assistant.

Nia's stomach dropped.
Her mind raced. Who had taken that photo? Who had posted it? How deep this betrayal went.
A cold realization settled in her bones. This wasn't gossip. It was sabotage.

And as she stared at the glowing screen, another notification appeared.
A new comment under the photo:

Looks like the Rebuild Project just fell apart.

The phone slipped from her hand, clattering against the concrete floor.
Nia pressed her back to the wall, her breath shaking as the words echoed in her mind.

Fell apart. Fell apart.

But somewhere beneath the fear, another voice rose. It was quiet, resolute, and familiar. Laneshia's voice from years ago:
Even when they bury you in lies, remember, seeds grow in the dark.

Nia lifted her head, eyes burning, the hum of the city below like a heartbeat.

She whispered, through clenched teeth,
"They want a scandal... but God's about to write a resurrection."

The stairwell door creaked open, footsteps echoing down the steps.
"Nia," a man's voice called softly.

Caleb.

She froze. Torn between anger, fear, and something dangerously like longing.

"Don't," she whispered again, her voice breaking.

But the door clicked shut behind him.

And in that moment, standing between fire and silence, Nia realized nothing about her life would ever be the same again.

9

The Weight of Witness

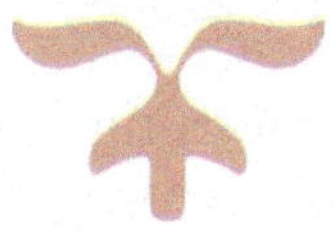

The stairwell hummed with the low moan of pipes and the city's pulse outside. Car horns, faint music, and the far-off cry of sirens. Nia stood frozen, her back to the cool concrete wall, as Caleb descended the last step. His presence filled the small space. He stood tall, steady, his expression taut with concern and something unspoken.

"Nia," he said quietly, "please don't walk away like this."

Her throat tightened. "You shouldn't have followed me."

"I couldn't let you face that alone."

She let out a shaky laugh. "Face what? The whispering saints or the pastor who just benched me from my own ministry?" Her voice cracked. "They made me into a headline, Caleb. Like all the work I've done, all the healing, all the lives changed, means nothing because somebody wanted to stir a rumor."

He took a step closer, careful, as if she were something fragile. "People are talking because they don't understand strength in a woman like you. They see confidence and call it vanity. They see compassion and call it temptation. It's not you that's the problem. It's their fear."

The words pierced something soft inside her.
She turned her face away, blinking back tears. "That fear might cost me everything I built."

He hesitated, then reached down and picked up her phone from the floor. "Then rebuild again," he said gently. "You've done it before."

That was the kind of thing he always said. Simple, but sharp enough to break through despair. Nia swallowed hard, staring at his hand. The one holding her phone then at his other, which hung at his side like he wanted to reach for her but didn't dare.

"Thank you," she murmured, taking the phone. Their fingers brushed and there was a spark that startled them both.

Silence swelled between them.
And beneath it, that unspoken current. The one she'd tried to deny for months.

She took a step back. "You need to go, Caleb. The more they see us together, the worse it gets."

His jaw tightened. "I'm not going to let fear dictate what's right. What's right is standing with you when everyone else runs."

Nia met his eyes. Steady, brown, alive with conviction. "And what happens when that ruins your reputation too? You're the associate pastor, Caleb. They'll come for you next."

He smiled sadly. "They already have. But I care more about truth than image."

For a moment, everything slowed. The air was thick with tension, her pulse loud in her ears.
He stepped closer, close enough that she could smell his cologne, cedar and something warm, familiar.

"Nia," he said softly, "I know what they're saying. But I also know what's real. And I'm not walking away from that."

Her breath hitched.
She wanted to believe him. To believe that conviction could outrun gossip. But she also knew what church politics could do to people. She'd seen it break stronger hearts than hers.

"You don't know what you're risking," she whispered.
He held her gaze. "I do. And it's worth it."

Something inside her trembled. The urge to cry, to collapse into the comfort he offered, battled the part of her that still remembered every wound disguised as love, every sermon that turned into judgment. She took a step back, hugging herself.

“I need space,” she said finally. “If I don’t hear God clearly right now, I’ll start listening to my hurt instead.”

He nodded slowly, pain flickering across his face. “Then I’ll give you that space. But just know, I’m still praying for you. Every day.”

He turned and climbed the stairs, his footsteps echoing into the silence above.

When he was gone, Nia exhaled shakily and sank onto the cold step. For a long time, she just sat there. The leader who’d been silenced, the believer wrestling with disbelief. Her hands trembled as she scrolled through her phone. The post was still spreading! Likes, shares, hateful comments. Some defending her, most tearing her apart.

Then, beneath it all, one familiar name appeared in the comments — *Taneshia Monroe.*
Her heart lurched.

The comment read:

“When you’re called, you’ll always be criticized before you’re crowned. Stand still and let God fight the lie.”

Nia covered her mouth, tears spilling over. Even from miles away, her mentor still knew how to send truth straight into her soul.

That night, she didn’t go home. Instead, she drove aimlessly through Atlanta’s glowing streets until the sky bruised purple. Finally, she parked outside her old childhood church, the same one she’d sworn she’d never return to after they’d shamed her years ago for "not looking holy enough." The sign out front was cracked, the building smaller than she remembered.

Inside, the sanctuary was dark except for the soft light spilling through stained glass. Dust motes floated in the air like memories.
Nia knelt at the altar. The same wooden rail where she'd once cried as a teenager after her first heartbreak and she prayed. Not eloquently. Not the kind of prayer you post about.
Just a raw whisper:

"God… if You're still in this, tell me how to stand when I'm tired of being misunderstood."

She waited. Minutes passed. Nothing but the hum of the old air vents.

Then, somewhere deep inside, a voice that wasn't her own:
You're not misunderstood — you're being refined.

Her tears came harder.
Because refinement hurts more than rejection — it burns what can't stay.

Two days later, she showed up at The Rebuild Project headquarters. Some staff avoided eye contact. Others hugged her wordlessly. The news had spread too far to ignore, but Nia moved with a calm that surprised even herself. She met with the board, answered questions, and refused to let her voice tremble.

When one woman asked if she would resign, Nia looked her in the eye.
"No," she said simply. "You can't fire obedience."

By that evening, the gossip had begun to lose its fire. Truth, quiet and steady, was beginning to push through the smoke.

But peace rarely lasts long.

Late that night, Nia's phone buzzed again. Another message from the same anonymous number.
This time, no words. Just a video file.

She hesitated, then pressed play.
The footage showed her office. Empty, except for a shadow moving across the wall. Then the camera turned toward her desk. Someone's hand placed a folded letter on top. The video ended abruptly.

A note taped to her office door the next morning confirmed what she feared, block letters scrawled in black ink:

"You should've stayed silent. Some people aren't meant to lead."

Nia's breath caught.
This wasn't just gossip anymore.
It was war.

And as she stood there, gripping the note, the church bells across the street began to ring. Slow, solemn...echoing through the early morning air.

Something told her the next sound she'd hear would change everything.

10

The Breaking and the Blooming

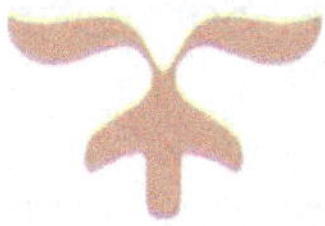

The note stayed on Nia's desk like a bruise she couldn't cover. For a long time, she just stared at it, the words vibrating in her mind. *You should've stayed silent.*

She'd spent too many years learning to speak after silence. Too many nights praying through the ache of being misunderstood. And now, after everything she'd survived, someone wanted to drag her back into the shadows.

Not this time.

She folded the note carefully, slipped it into her bag, and walked out of her office. The morning sun poured through the front windows of The Rebuild Project, streaking the polished floor with light. It reminded her of something Laneshia used to say: *When God exposes darkness, don't flinch. Just stand still and let Him turn the light on.*

She was done flinching.

By noon, she was at the church again, walking straight through the fellowship hall where the weekly leadership luncheon buzzed with polite chatter. The moment she stepped in, conversation stopped. Forks clinked against plates. Someone whispered her name.

She walked right up to Sister Marla.

“Can we talk?” Nia asked, her tone even but edged with resolve.

Marla looked startled then quickly recovered, adjusting her pearl earrings. “Of course, dear. Though this isn’t really the time—”

“It is,” Nia said, cutting her off. “It’s exactly the time.”

The pastor, seated at the head of the table, cleared his throat. “Sister Daniels, if this is about—”

“It is,” she said again, her voice calm but carrying through the room. “Because this isn’t just about me. It’s about integrity and the example we set for the women we claim to mentor.”

She reached into her bag and placed the folded note on the table. “This was left in my office. And before anyone says I’m overreacting, there’s also video footage of someone placing something on my desk last night.”

A ripple of murmurs spread through the room.

Marla's smile faltered. "Surely you're not implying—"

"I'm not implying anything," Nia said, steady. "I'm stating facts. The handwriting matches a note I received days ago from someone connected to your assistant."

Marla's cheeks flushed. "That's a serious accusation."

"So is sabotaging another woman's ministry," Nia replied, her voice quiet but unyielding. "You've been spreading lies under the disguise of righteousness. But God doesn't anoint manipulation."

Gasps. Someone dropped a fork.

The pastor looked between them, frowning. "Is this true, Marla?"

Marla's lips pressed into a thin line. "I only wanted to protect the church's reputation."

"By destroying someone else's?" Nia asked softly. "You don't protect the house of God by burning down one of its rooms."

For a long moment, no one spoke. Then Marla's shoulders slumped. "I didn't post the picture," she muttered, eyes glistening. "But... I told someone to keep an eye on you. I didn't know it would go that far."

Nia inhaled slowly. Not in triumph or satisfaction. Just release. "Thank you for telling the truth."

Pastor Lyle rose. "Sister Marla, we'll discuss this privately. Sister Nia, I owe you an apology. I should've trusted your integrity."

Nia nodded. "Thank you, Pastor. I accept your apology but I'm not here for validation. I'm here because this ministry, this church, and these women deserve better than fear dressed up as holiness."

She turned to leave, but the pastor called after her. "Where are you going?"

"To do what God told me to do," she said simply. "Rebuild."

That evening, she returned to The Rebuild Project. Her staff gathered in the meeting room both hesitant and uncertain. Nia stood before them, not as a victim, but as a leader refined by fire.

"I know some of you are afraid," she began. "You've seen what happens when people twist good things. But let me tell you something Laneshia once told me: *If the lie spreads faster than the truth, just wait. The truth's roots go deeper.*"

A few people smiled through tears.

She continued, voice firm: "We're not shutting down. We're not hiding. We're going to keep rebuilding. One woman, one story, one soul at a time."

The room erupted in quiet applause. Some hugged her; others just nodded with renewed strength.

When the meeting ended, she stepped outside into the soft dusk. The air was warm, tinged with jasmine from the church garden next door. And there, leaning against his car, was Caleb.

He looked different. Tired, maybe, but his eyes were the same as always. Steady and kind.

"I heard what happened," he said. "I wanted to make sure you were okay."

"I'm fine," she said, managing a small smile. "Better than fine, actually. God showed out."

He chuckled. "He usually does when we stop trying to help Him."

They stood there a moment in easy silence, watching the sun dip below the skyline. The air between them hummed with something gentle but real. Not the uncertain tension of before, but peace laced with possibility.

Caleb spoke first. "You ever think maybe all this, the chaos, the conflict, was just preparation?"

"For what?" she asked softly.

He looked at her then, not as a rumor, not as a leader, but as a woman. "For partnership. In purpose. Maybe even in more than that."

Her heart skipped. "You sure you know what you're saying? I come with... complications."

He smiled. "So does faith. But I think both are worth it."

Nia exhaled, a soft laugh escaping. "You sound like Laneshia."

"Then I'm in good company," he said.

The streetlight flickered on above them, haloing their faces in soft amber.
Nia looked up at the wide, open, infinite night sky.
"Maybe this time," she said quietly, "I won't run from what's good just because it's not perfect."

Caleb nodded. "That sounds like growth."

"It sounds like grace," she replied.

They stood there a long time, not needing to fill the silence. For once, it wasn't heavy. It was holy.

Weeks later, The Rebuild Project held its biggest conference yet. Women from across the country filled the sanctuary. Nia stepped to the pulpit, not as someone defending her worth, but as someone walking in it.

She spoke of forgiveness, of faith, of the quiet miracles that happen when women refuse to shrink. And when she looked out at the crowd, she saw faces shining with recognition. The beauty of broken things made whole.

Afterward, as music filled the room, Caleb met her at the edge of the stage. He didn't say anything. Just reached for her hand. This time, she didn't pull away.

Outside, the same concrete courtyard where she once stood in shame now bloomed with flowers planted by the women she'd mentored. Roses pushing through cracks, defying the odds. One pink rose in particular stood taller than the rest.

Nia smiled, whispering to herself, "Laneshia was right. Seeds grow in the dark."

The wind stirred, warm and full of promise. And for the first time in a long while, Nia didn't just feel rebuilt. She felt reborn.

Epilogue – Still Blooming

One year later.

Atlanta shimmered under a late-spring sun, the kind of warm brightness that made the whole city hum. The Rebuild Project had grown beyond anyone's imagination. New branches opening in three cities, mentorship programs for teen girls, community kitchens run by women who once sat in Nia's support groups. The same building that once held her shame now pulsed with joy and purpose.

The walls of her office were covered with photos with faces of women laughing, crying, and rebuilding. In the center hung a framed quote from Laneshia, written in her looping handwriting:

You don't have to prove you're chosen. Just walk like it.

Nia smiled at it every morning before meetings, before prayer, before the noise of leadership began.

A gentle knock sounded at her door.
"Come in," she said.

Caleb stepped inside, a soft grin on his face. "They're all set downstairs. You ready, Mrs. Morris?"

She looked up, feigning surprise. "You still calling me that like it's new?"

He laughed. "Still sounds good, though."

Nia shook her head, unable to hide her smile. They'd married quietly six months earlier. A small ceremony at sunset, surrounded by the women of Rebuild and a few close friends. She thought about something Laneshia had told her before, "You can always tell it's God when restoration outshines reputation."

The past year hadn't been perfect. They'd weathered old rumors, long nights, growing pains of ministry but through it all, they'd learned what partnership in purpose really looked like. Not rescuing each other but respecting the journey that had shaped them both.

Caleb took her hand. "You sure you want to talk today? You don't have to."

She squeezed his fingers. "No. I do. Somebody out there needs to hear that healing isn't a myth."

Together they walked downstairs to the community hall. The room was full. Rows of folding chairs, women of every age and story gathered for the first annual **Rebuild Women's Gathering**. The air was alive with expectancy.

As Nia stepped up to the podium, she spotted a few familiar faces, one was Sister Marla, sitting quietly in the back. Her expression was softer now, her hands folded in her lap. Redemption had a way of humbling everyone it touched.

Nia opened her notes, then closed them again.
She didn't need them.

"Good morning, family," she began. Her voice carried warmth and quiet authority. "When this ministry started, it was just a handful of women sitting in a basement, trying to believe that broken things could still bloom. We didn't know what we were building, we just knew God wasn't done."

A murmur of *amens* rippled through the crowd.

She continued, "I used to think being misunderstood was a curse. But now I see it was a classroom. Every lie, every rumor, every setback. It all taught me to lean on truth instead of approval. And truth don't need permission to rise."

The audience clapped, a few women wiping tears.

Nia smiled through her own. "So, if you're here today feeling like people don't see you, good! They're not supposed to. God's shaping you in the dark so your bloom won't depend on their light."

Behind her, a screen lit up with the Rebuild logo. A single pink rose breaking through concrete. The room fell quiet, reverent.

"I stand here not because I was perfect," she said, her voice softening, "but because grace kept finding me even when I tried to hide. And that same grace is waiting for you."

She paused, looking out across the sea of faces. "You're not disqualified. You're not forgotten. You're just getting started."

When the applause finally settled, Caleb stepped onto the stage, slipping an arm around her shoulders. She leaned into him. Not for support, but in shared peace.

As the choir began to sing, Nia looked up at the rafters where sunlight filtered through the windows, scattering beams across the crowd. Dust danced in the glow like tiny fragments of heaven.

And in that moment, she thought of Laneshia. The first time she'd sat across from her years ago, scared and searching. The baton had been passed. The circle was complete.

Nia whispered a prayer under her breath:
"Thank You for the misunderstandings that led me home."

Outside, in the courtyard, the pink roses were in full bloom. Bright against the gray concrete, roots deep, and petals open to the sky.

And as laughter drifted from inside the building, it was clear...
The rebuilding never ended.
It just kept growing.

Acknowledgments

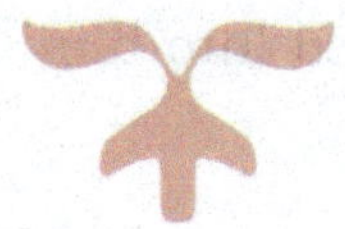

To the One who makes beauty from ashes,
thank You for every door You opened through faith,
even when I couldn't see the way.

To my *three roses*,
you are my quiet strength and constant reminder
that love grows even through the cracks.
You inspire me to keep writing, keep believing, and
keep blooming.
You know who you are.

To every woman who has ever felt unseen, unheard,
or misunderstood,
this story is for you.
May it remind you that you are never disqualified
from grace,
and that rebuilding is always possible.

To Chattelle,
my incredible creative partner and sounding board.
Thank you for helping me bring this story to life
with patience, clarity, and care.
You made the process lighter and the vision brighter.

And to every reader holding this book,
thank you for walking with Nia and me
through every twist, tear, and triumph.
My hope is that you finish this story
believing in your own restoration, one bloom at a time.

Author's Note

When I first began *Misunderstandings of Nia*, I thought I was writing fiction. But somewhere between the sentences, I realized I was writing my own healing.

Like Nia, I've known what it feels like to be misunderstood. To carry purpose wrapped in pain. To serve faithfully and still be questioned. This story came from real seasons of silence, surrender, and grace that only God could orchestrate.

Through Nia's journey, I wanted to show that redemption doesn't always arrive in grand moments. Sometimes it comes quietly through the rebuilding of trust, the rediscovery of worth, and the refusal to give up.

If you've ever been broken, judged, or counted out, let this be your reminder. *You are still becoming.* God hasn't forgotten you. The same light that guided Nia home is waiting for you, too.

Keep rebuilding. Keep blooming. Even when they don't understand your soil, your roots are deeper than they know.

With all my heart,

Laadie Ohh

"Where the Bloom Begins"

They said she was broken
because they only saw the cracks.
But God saw the light slipping through,
the quiet glow of a woman learning
how to become her own dawn.

They named her by her storms,
misread her silence
and misunderstood her rising.
But she learned that truth isn't proven,
it's lived.

So, she walked forward anyway,
carrying every rumor, every whisper,
every shadow that tried to claim her.
And somewhere between the bending
and the breaking,
she found her bloom.

Not in the sunlight of approval,
but in the soil of becoming.
Deep roots, soft petals
A strength she no longer had to explain.

This is for every woman
who was misjudged before understood,
who learned to breathe again
before she was believed,

who dared to grow in places
that were never meant to hold her.

You are not your misunderstandings.
You are the lesson, the rising,
the bloom after the storm.

And grace...
quiet, steady, and relentless...

is still writing your name
in places your pain could never reach.

Made in the USA
Coppell, TX
02 January 2026

67621270R00066